Mauga
now 38

My Picture Encyclopedia

Designed by Annie Simpson
Written by Charles Phillips
Illustrations by Paula Metcalf
Consultant: Dr S Beaumont

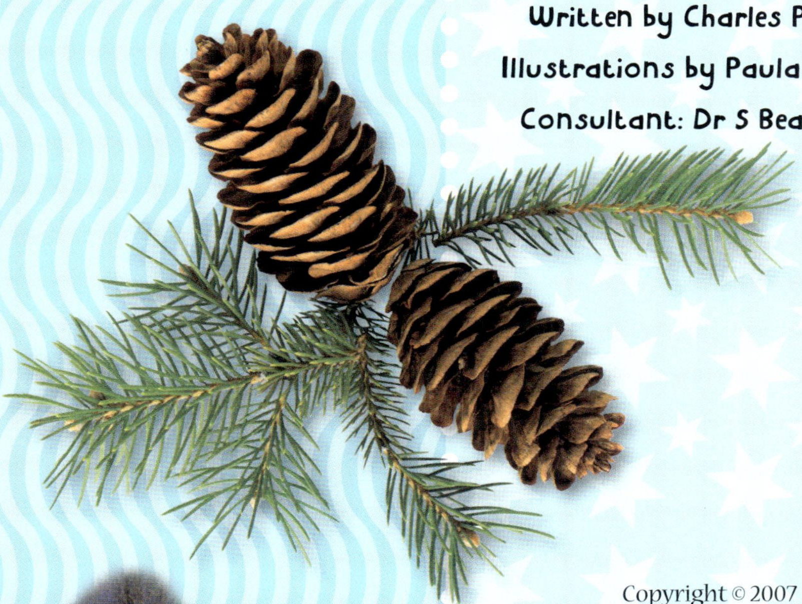

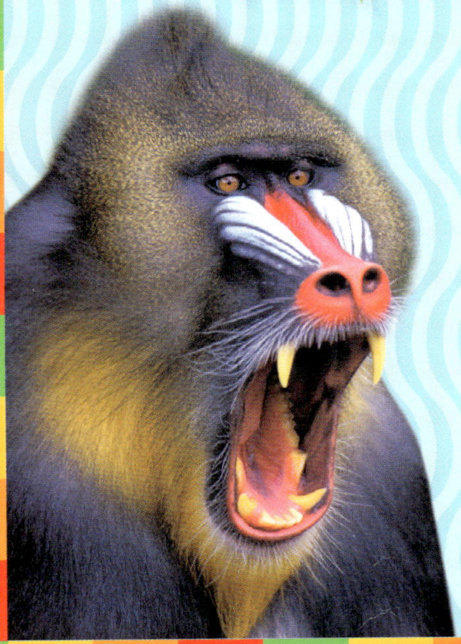

Copyright © 2007

make believe ideas ltd
27 Castle Street, Berkhamsted,
Hertfordshire, HP4 2DW.

make
believe
ideas

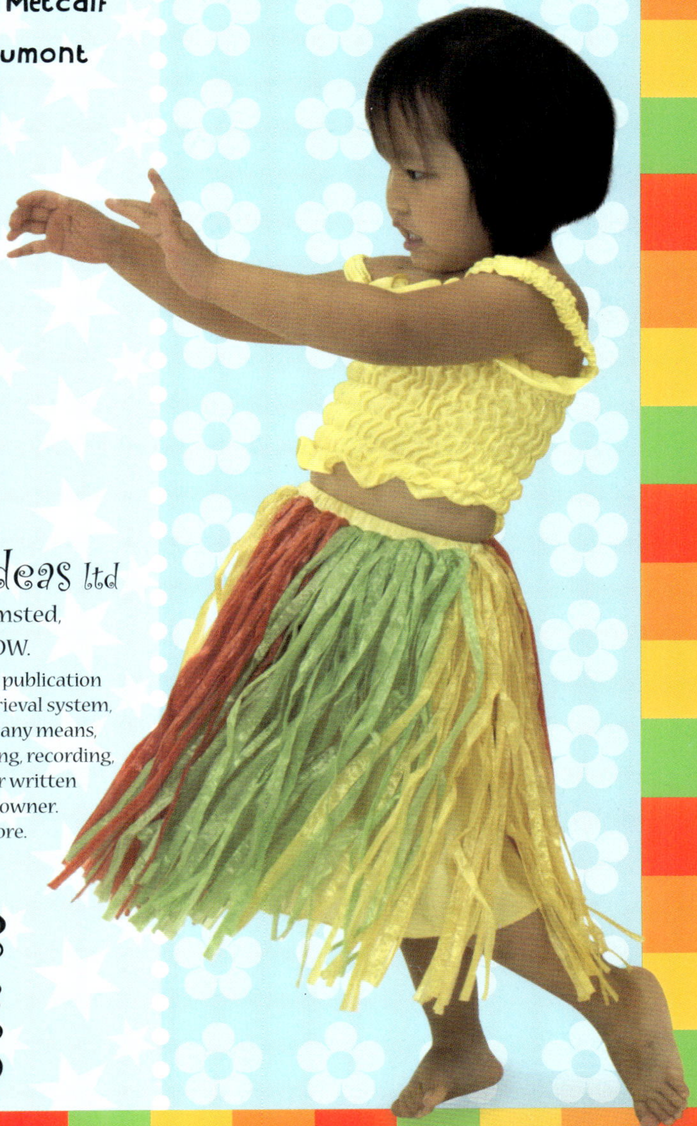

YOUR BODY

Your body   4

Heart and lungs   6

Your digestion   7

Skin   8

Hair   9

SENSES

Seeing   10

Hearing   11

Tasting   12

Smelling   13

ALL ABOUT YOU

Staying healthy   14

Eating well   16

Family   18

PLANTS AND ANIMALS

Plants   20

Trees   22

Insects   24

Birds   25

Pets   26

Farm animals   27

Wild animals   28

Sea animals   30

Animals in danger   32

CONTENTS

THE WORLD

In space 34

Continents and oceans 36

Volcanoes 38

Earthquakes 39

The Earth's landscapes 40

Seasons 42

Weather 44

RELIGIONS

Religions 46

Festivals 50

WHAT PEOPLE DO

Music 52

Entertainment 54

Jobs 56

TRAVEL

Travellers and explorers 58

Getting around 60

Delivering and rescuing 62

INDEX 64

Your body

Your bones support your body, and muscles pull the bones to make your body move. Your brain and nerves control your muscles.

X-ray

An X-ray is a kind of photograph that shows your bones.

The bones in your hand fit together like a jigsaw puzzle.

Bones

You have more than 200 bones inside you. They join together to form your skeleton. They get bigger as you grow taller.

skull

lower arm

upper arm

hip bone

kneecap

ribcage

thigh bone

shin bone

ankle bone

Ribcage

As well as supporting your body, your bones protect the soft organs inside you. Your ribcage protects your heart and lungs.

Joint

A **joint** is where two bones meet.

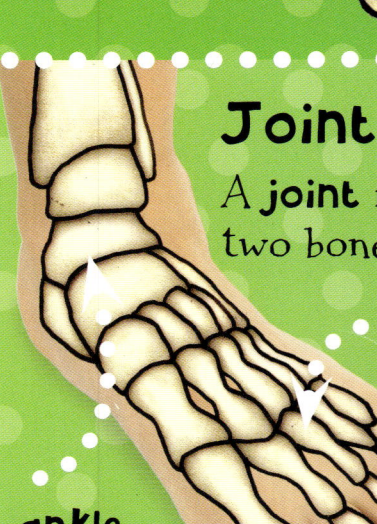

foot bones

ankle joint

Muscles

Exercising your muscles makes them strong and flexible. You have more than 600 muscles.

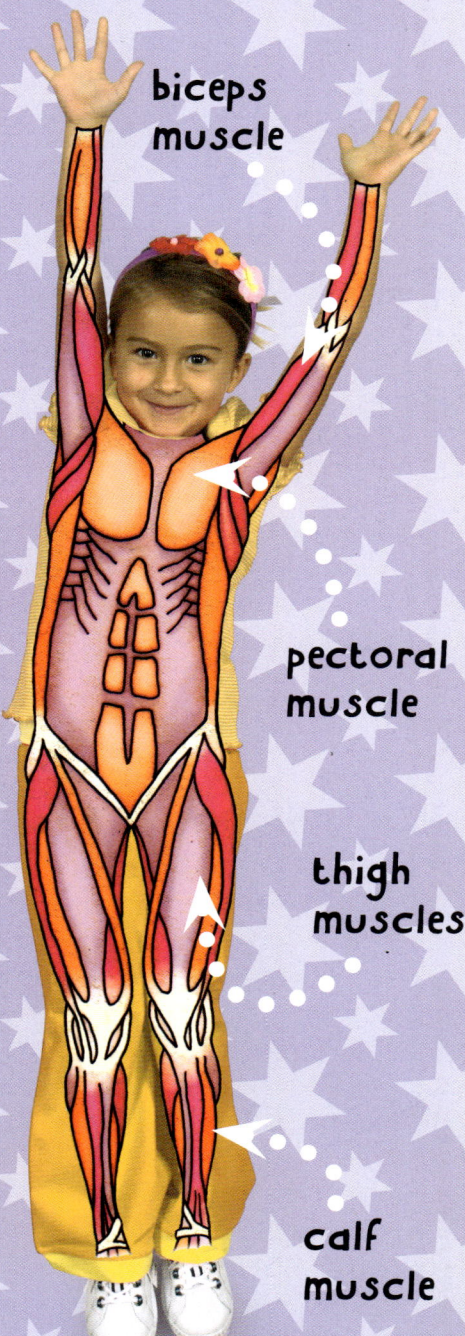

biceps muscle

pectoral muscle

thigh muscles

calf muscle

Tendons are like straps. They attach your muscles to your bones.

Brain and nerves

Your brain is small but powerful. You have one and a half times more brain cells than there are people in the whole world! Your brain controls your body. It sends and receives signals along your nerves.

Your brain's wrinkled surface makes it look like a big walnut.

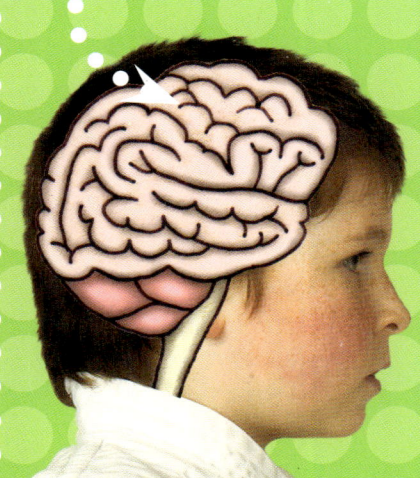

Nerves run down the **spinal cord** in your back

Reflex action

If you touch something sharp like a thorn on a cactus, your nerves make you pull away. This is a reflex action.

Thinking

You also use your brain for thinking, feeling and remembering.

Heart and lungs

Your lungs take in oxygen from the air. Your heart pumps blood around your body. The blood carries oxygen from your lungs all around your body.

Air enters your **lungs** through air tubes. In your lungs oxygen passes into your blood.

Your **heart** beats without a rest from the moment you are born until the end of your life.

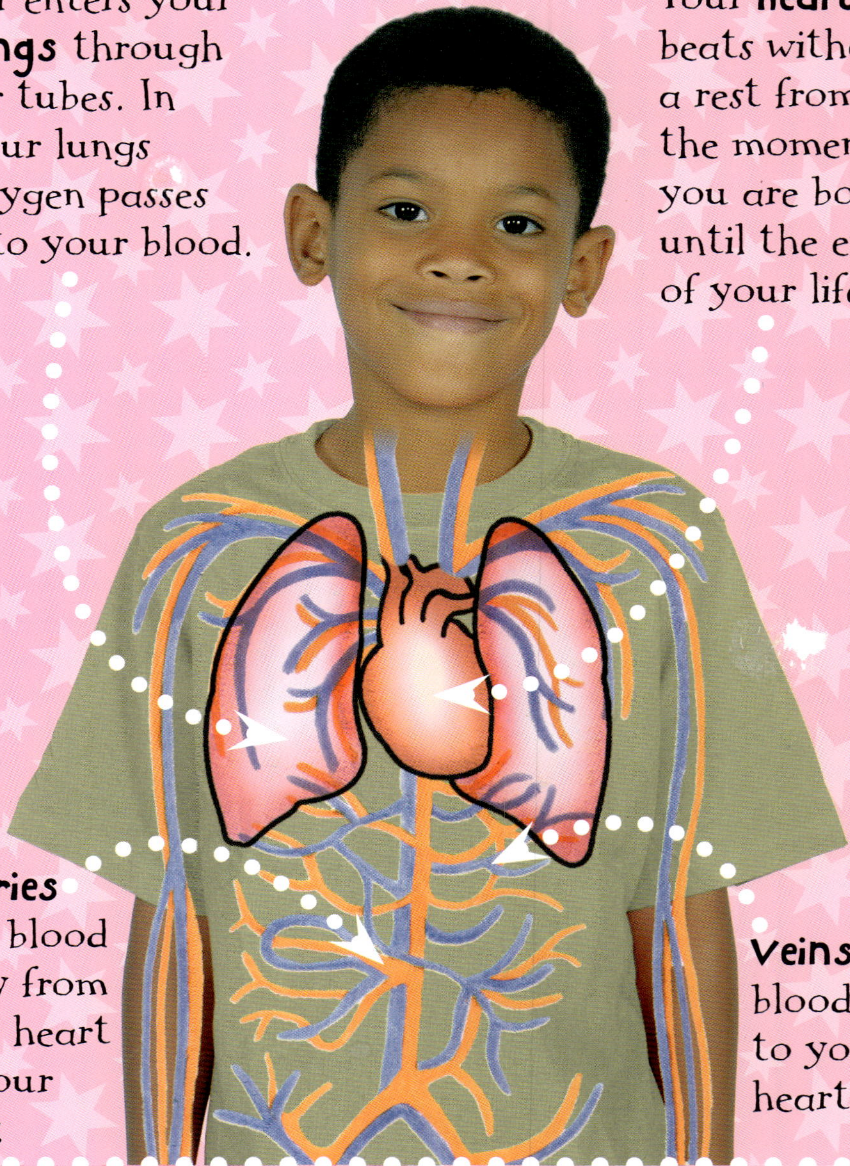

Heart

Your **heart** is a powerful muscle about as big as your fist. It beats 70 times a minute.

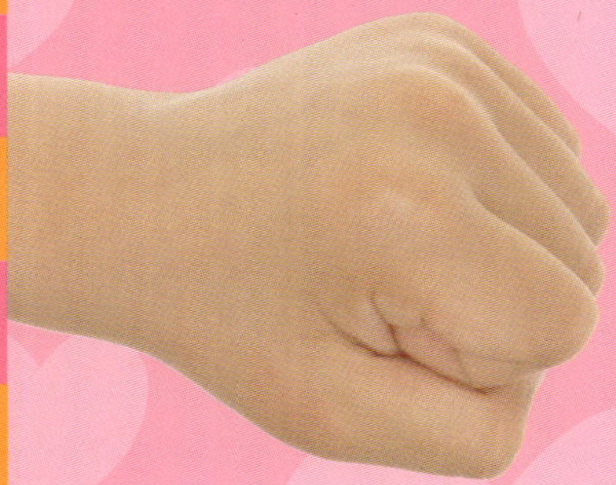

Arteries take blood away from your heart to your body.

Veins carry blood back to your heart.

Asthma

People with asthma sometimes find it hard to breathe. Muscles in the air tubes into their lungs get tight. They take a puff from an inhaler to relax the muscles, and then they can breathe more easily.

Panting

When you run or jump you need more oxygen, so you breathe in and out more quickly.

Your digestion

Your body takes the goodness it needs to be healthy out of the food you eat. Your stomach, intestines, liver and kidneys work together every day to do this.

Your **teeth** chew and grind food before you swallow it.

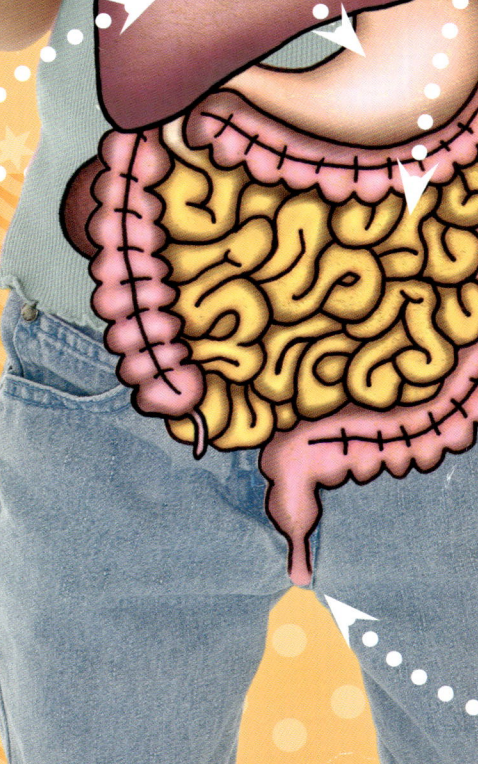

In your **small intestine**, your body absorbs food goodness into your blood.

Your **large intestine** holds the food that your body cannot digest.

Your **stomach** breaks up food into a thick soup.

Your **liver** does almost 500 jobs! The most important is to take food goodness from your blood and send it around your body. It also removes from your blood things that are not good for your body.

Your **kidneys,** which sit behind your intestine, take out liquid waste from your blood and make it into urine (wee).

The waste (poo) leaves your body here.

Skin

Your body is covered all over in skin. It is stretchy and tough. It keeps germs and water out, and stops you getting too hot.

Fingerprints

No two people have the same fingerprint. This is the pattern of ridges on the end of your finger.

Cuts

If you fall over and cut your skin, your blood cells clot and form a covering or scab over the cut. Then white blood cells attack any germs that have got in. A new layer of skin grows beneath the scab.

Sometimes we put a **plaster** on the cut to protect it.

Skin colour

The colour of your skin depends on how much dark colouring called melanin you have. Melanin helps prevent sunburn. It blocks out some of the sunlight.

Some of us have dark skin.

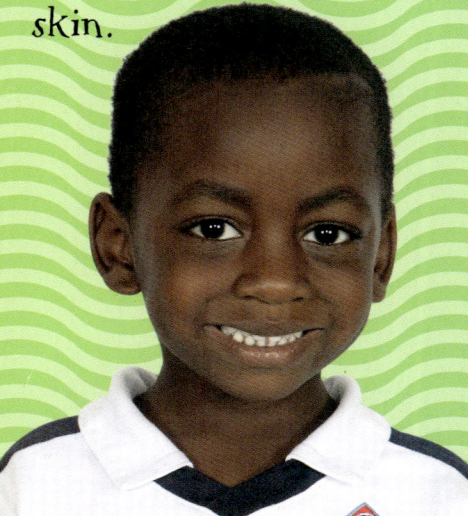

Some of us have light brown skin.

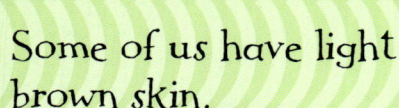

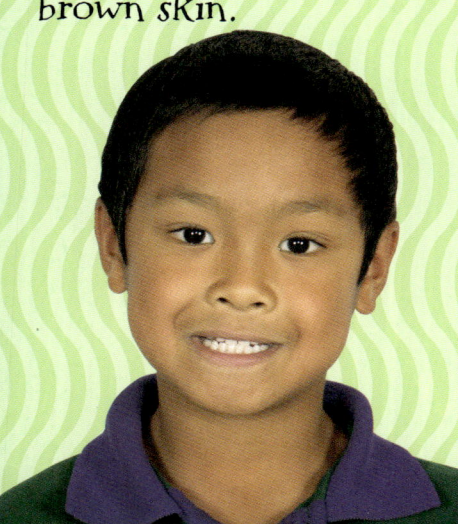

Some of us have very pale skin.

Sweating

When you are too hot, tiny holes in your skin let out sweat. As the sweat dries, it cools your body down.

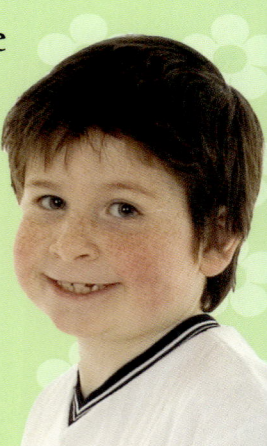

Hair

The hair on your head keeps off strong sunlight and helps you stay warm on cold days. Hair also helps protect your head against knocks.

You lose about 90 **hairs** every day! But so long as you stay healthy more hair grows all the time.

Some of us have ginger hair.

Some of us have dark, tightly curling hair.

Some of us have dark, wavy hair.

Some of us have blonde hair.

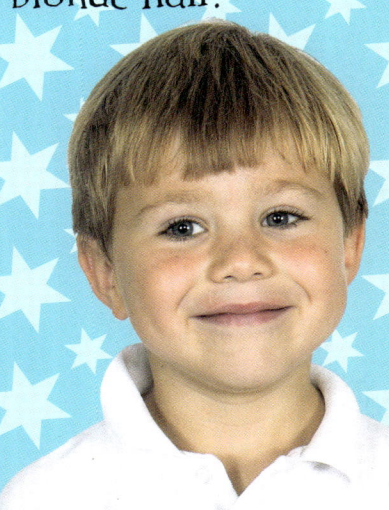

Seeing

You see with your eyes. When light enters your eyes, they send nerve messages to your brain to tell it what you are seeing.

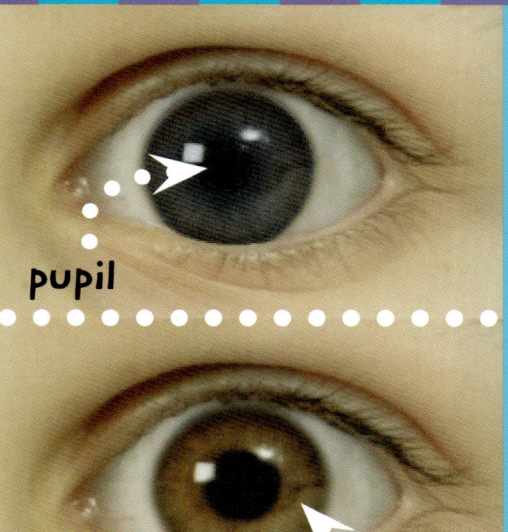

pupil

Pupil

The pupil is an opening in the centre of your eye. In the dark the pupil gets bigger to let in more light. On a bright day, the pupil gets smaller to let in less light.

The **iris** is the coloured part of your eye.

How you see

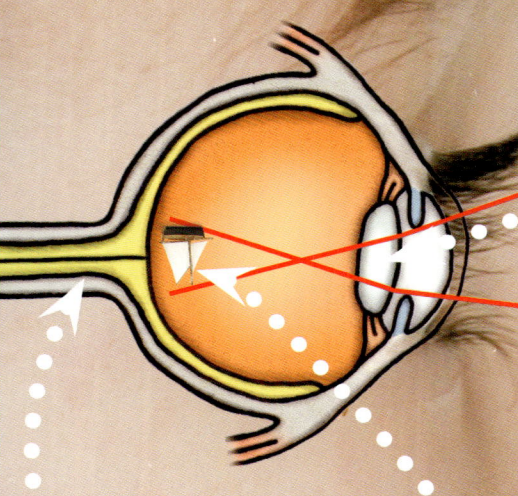

Light goes through the **lens** at the front of the eye onto the **retina**.

The image on the retina is **upside down**

A signal goes from the retina to the brain along the **optic nerve**. The brain translates the signal so you see things right way up.

Look after your eyes

Some people need to wear glasses to see clearly. If you need glasses, make sure you wear them.

10

Hearing

You hear with your ears. The ears respond to sound vibrations in the air. They turn the vibrations into nerve signals, and send them to your brain.

How you hear

Your **outer ear** catches sound vibrations in the air.

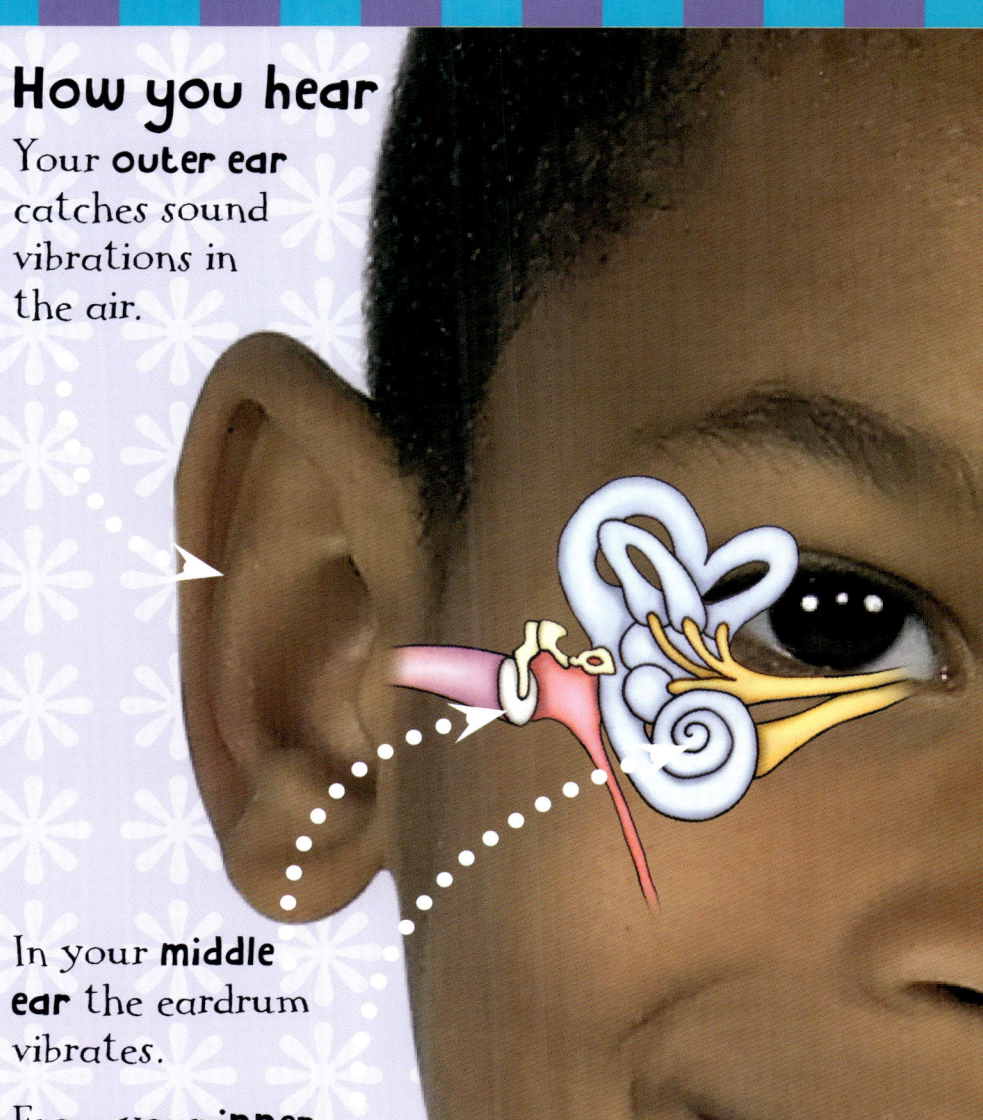

In your **middle ear** the eardrum vibrates.

From your **inner ear** nerve signals travel to the brain.

Handstand

Nerves like tiny hairs in your inner ear can tell whether you are upside down or the right way up.

Sounds we can't hear

Dogs and sea creatures like whales can hear high and low sounds that we can't hear.

"I feel dizzy!"

When you spin round, the nerves in your inner ear send confused messages to your brain. You feel dizzy because you think your head is still spinning even when you have stopped.

Tasting

You taste with your tongue. Tiny bumps on your tongue called taste buds respond to different tastes. You have 10,000 taste buds on your tongue!

How you taste

Different parts of your **tongue** are sensitive to different tastes.

bitter at the back

salty all over

sweet at the front

sour at the side

Bitter

The taste buds at the back of your tongue are sensitive to bitter tastes, like watercress or sprouts.

Salty

Taste buds all over your tongue respond to the flavour of potato crisps and other salty foods.

Sweet

You taste sweet foods like iced buns with the taste buds at the tip of your tongue.

Sour

Sour foods like lemon stimulate the taste buds at the sides of your tongue.

Smelling

You smell with your nose. Hairs at the very top inside of your nose are sensitive to smells in the air. Nerves send signals from your nose to your brain.

Blocked nose

Your sense of smell helps you taste things. When you have a cold, and your nose is blocked, you can't taste things very well.

How you smell

You suck air onto the sensitive area at the top of your nose to smell something well.

You breathe in through your **nostrils**.

Strawberries smell good.

Touching

When you touch things, nerves in your skin send signals to your brain. You can tell if the things are hot or cold, wet or dry, hard or soft, prickly or smooth.

hot

soft

cold

prickly

13

Staying healthy

The best ways to stay healthy are to take exercise, keep clean and eat a good mixture of foods. Make sure you get enough rest.

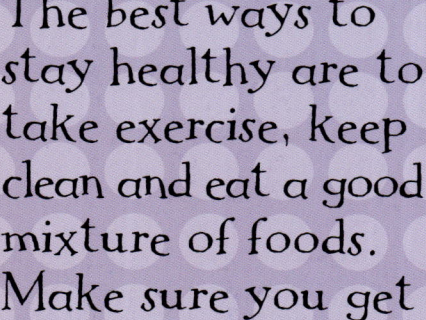

ball

When you practise **throwing** or **catching** a ball, it makes your arms stronger.

Taking exercise

Exercise is fun – and it's good for you! It keeps your muscles and your heart in good shape and your bones strong.

Martial arts train your body and your mind to be wide awake.

As you get better at martial arts you change the colour of your belt. The best people usually wear black belts.

People wear special white suits to do martial arts.

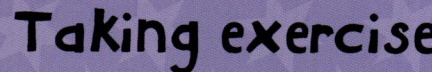

Playing **football** helps you get good at running.

football shirt

Skipping improves your balance.

rope

Whizzing around on a **scooter** is great fun. Are you sure you know how to stop?

Keeping clean

Wash off dirt and germs – they can make you ill.

Eating well

Your body needs a mixture of foods. Don't eat too many sweets!

Drinking

Don't dry up! Remember to drink plenty of liquids.

milk

Sharing problems

Don't bottle things up! Tell someone you trust if you are worried.

Brushing your teeth

Look after your teeth – brush them both morning and evening.

toothbrush

Care in the sun

Cover up or use sun lotion in bright sunlight.

hat

sunglasses

Getting enough sleep

Your body repairs itself when you are asleep. You feel at your best after a good night's rest.

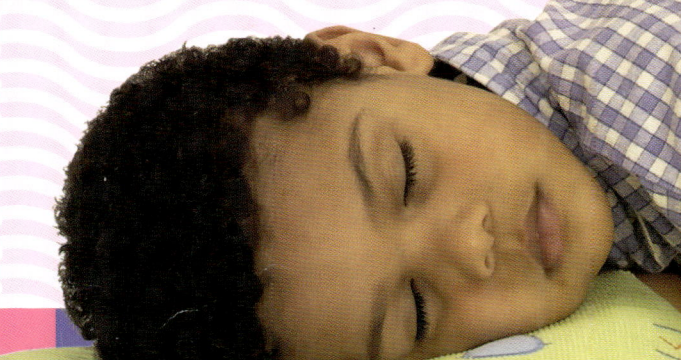

Eating well

To keep healthy, your body needs a mixture of different types of food. Try not to eat too much of any one type.

Vitamins and minerals

Vitamins and minerals in fruit and vegetables keep your body working.

tomatoes

bananas

pears

A balanced diet

This plate shows approximately the amount of carbohydrates, fruit and vegetables, protein and fat that you should eat.

protein

fat

carbohydrate

fruit and vegetables

Protein

Protein in meat, eggs, cheese, milk, nuts or avocados helps your body grow.

Carbohydrates

Carbohydrates such as potatoes, bread and pasta give you energy.

Fats

Fats also give you energy. Try to eat only a little fat, because too much is bad for you.

Fibre

Fibre in wholewheat bread, cereal or a banana helps your digestion work.

Water

Your body needs plenty of water. Try to drink at least six glasses every day.

A day's work

It can take up to 24 hours to digest a meal fully.

On the move

Eating well gives you energy. Keeping active helps you stay healthy.

Big appetite

The amount of food that a teenager or a grown-up eats in a year weighs about the same as a small car!

Going up!

To grow tall, you need vitamins from fruit and vegetables. Calcium from milk and cheese is also good for growing. It gives you strong bones.

Family

You probably live with your mum and dad and perhaps your brother or sister. You see other people in your family – like cousins – now and then.

Grandma

Your grandma is your mum's mum or your dad's mum.

Grandad

Your grandad is your dad's dad or your mum's dad.

Aunty and uncle

When your aunty and uncle visit, everyone has fun!

Mum and Dad

Some people live with their mum or their dad and others live with both parents. Your mum and dad work hard to make sure you are safe and happy.

Cousins

Your cousins are your aunty and uncle's children.

Brother

It's great to have a brother to talk to and to play with!

Sister

You're lucky if you have a sister to help you make up stories, jokes and games!

Family likeness

You can often tell when people are members of the same family because they look alike.

Brothers and sisters often have similar eyes or a face that is the same shape.

Having a baby

If your mum has another baby then you will have a new sister or brother! Babies live inside their mums for nine months before they are born. It's exciting to help look after a new baby.

Growing up

As you get older, you can do more and more things for yourself.

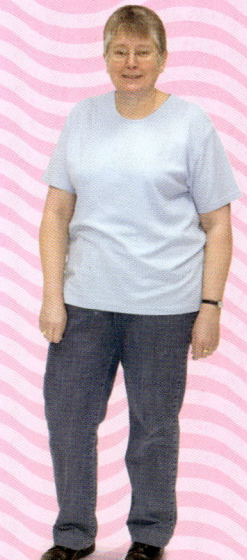

Plants

People need plants to live. We use plants for food and to make clothes. Plants also release oxygen into the air, and people need oxygen to breathe.

Seeds

Most plants make seeds from which new plants can grow.

Peas are seeds.

Spores

Some plants make tiny spores instead of seeds. The spores become new plants.

Moss grows by making spores.

Parts of a plant

Flowers attract insects, birds and other creatures to help make the plant's seeds and fruits.

The **leaves** make sap, the plant's food.

The **stem** supports the other parts of the plant.

To grow, plants need sunlight, water and air.

The **roots** hold the plant in the ground and take in water from the earth.

How plants make food

The leaves absorb the energy in sunlight and use it to make sap (food) from water and a gas called carbon dioxide in the air. As part of this process, the plant releases oxygen.

Chlorophyll (green colour) in the leaf absorbs energy.

Birds and insects come to flowers to drink a sweet liquid called **nectar**.

Sticky **pollen** in the flowers attaches to their body or legs.

How plants make seeds

Most plants cannot make seeds on their own. Birds and insects move pollen from one flower to a second one. The second flower uses the pollen to make seeds.

They carry it to another flower.

Plants that do not make seeds

Some plants can turn parts of themselves into new plants. A potato is a swollen root of the potato plant. If you don't dig it up, it will turn into a new potato plant.

potatoes

Fruits

Many plants produce fruits, like apples and pears. Inside the fruits are the plant's seeds. Nuts like the walnut and the hazelnut are fruits.

apple

pear

walnut

How seeds grow

A seed splits open and a **root** grows down into the soil.

A green **shoot** grows up from the root.

21

Trees

Trees have a thick wooden stem called a trunk. They grow tall and get plenty of sunlight. They can live a long time – some redwoods are 2,000 years old!

Blossom

Some fruit trees grow flowers called blossom.

Changing colours

Many trees lose their leaves in autumn. Before they fall off, the leaves turn red, orange or yellow.

How old is it?

You can tell a tree's age by counting the number of rings in the trunk.

Seeds and nuts

Trees grow seeds from which new trees can grow. In some trees, the seeds are inside nuts.

horse chestnut

sweet chestnut

Bark

The thick outer skin of the tree is called the bark.

Palm trees

Palm trees have thin trunks and large, fringed leaves that we call fronds. Usually palm trees grow in hot places. Coconuts and dates grow on palm trees.

palm frond

Evergreen trees

Some trees stay green all year round. We call them evergreen trees. They usually have needles rather than leaves and grow cones and berries. Evergreens normally grow in cold places. You often see them covered in snow.

Broad-leaved trees

Trees like oaks and beech trees have broad leaves. In autumn the leaves fall, and the trees have bare branches in winter before new leaves grow in spring. We also call them deciduous trees.

oak-tree acorn

oak leaf

pine cone

Insects

Most insects have six legs and many have wings. They often use long feelers to smell and touch things. Some insects can taste food using their feet.

Ladybird

black spots

leg

Ants

Ants live together in big groups known as colonies.

Body parts

All insects have three parts to their body. This insect is a beetle.

abdomen

head

thorax

Butterflies

Mother butterflies lay eggs. Caterpillars hatch from the eggs. The caterpillars eat and eat, then cover themselves up. Slowly they change completely and come out as butterflies.

antenna

butterfly

caterpillar

legs

wing

Fly

Bee

Creepy-crawlies

Are snails and millipedes insects? Do they have six legs? Do they have three parts to their body?

snail

millipede

Spiders are not insects. They have eight legs, not six.

Birds

Birds are the only animals that have feathers. There are thousands of types of bird. They live all over the world. All birds have wings, but not all birds can fly.

Ostrich

Ostriches can run very fast but they cannot fly.

long legs

Penguin

Penguins live in freezing Antarctica. They can't fly but they use their wings for swimming.

Eagle

wide wings

talons or claws

A nest of eggs

Baby birds hatch from **eggs**.

Owl

Owls have large eyes and very good hearing. They hunt at night.

Duck

waterproof feathers

Parrot

Parrots live in the trees of the rainforest.

Pets

We keep pet animals at home. Hamsters live in cages, and puppies have baskets. Rabbits and tortoises need to live in your garden or yard.

Goldfish

eye

fin

Budgie

perch

tail feather

Guinea pig

fur

Hamster

Hamsters run on a wheel in their cage.

Kitten

whiskers

ear

Tortoise

Always wash your hands after handling your tortoise. Some tortoises can live to be 100 years old.

hard shell

Puppy

You need to train your puppy. This means teaching it to behave well. You can start training it when it is about four months old.

Rabbit

Rabbits have long ears. They like eating grass and other plants.

Farm animals

All these animals live on the farm. The farmer gets up early every day to milk the cows, and to make sure that the other animals are safe and well fed.

Horse

Horses are strong. They pull the farmer's cart.

Chicks

fluffy feathers

beak

Goose

webbed feet

long neck

Pig

To keep cool, pigs roll in mud. A pig will eat almost anything. He sniffs out food with his snout.

snout

Goat

Farmers make delicious cheese from goats' milk.

Sheep

People make wool from a sheep's coat.

Cockerel

Cock-a-doodle-do! The call of a cockerel wakes up the farmyard in the morning.

Cow

Some farmers keep cows for their milk.

Wild animals

Animals in the wild need to be strong and alert. They have to find their own food. Sometimes they have to fight with or run away from other animals.

Snake

A snake's skin has dry scales.

zebra

Zebras are white with black stripes.

Bear

long shaggy fur

strong back leg

sharp claws

Wolf

thick coat

paw

Alligator

Alligators have very strong jaws and sharp teeth.

sharp tooth

Mandrill

eye

red nose

Lion

mane

tail

Lions love to eat! They can get through 34kg (75lb) of meat in one meal – that's the same as 300 quarter-pounder hamburgers!

Gazelle

horns

Gazelles live in herds on plains and grasslands.

Wallaby

thick coat

A wallaby is a smaller form of kangaroo.

Cheetah

A cheetah can run three times as fast as the quickest Olympic athlete.

spotted coat

Monkey

baby

Most monkeys live in trees. They are great at jumping and climbing!

long arm

Elephant

Elephants have huge ears and very good hearing. They live in jungles or grasslands.

large ear

tail

trunk

Giraffe

bony horn

Giraffes are tall enough to eat leaves at the very top of tall trees.

Sea animals

In the ocean beautifully coloured fish live among sharks, squid and other sea creatures. Many feed on underwater plants. Others are hunters.

Stingray

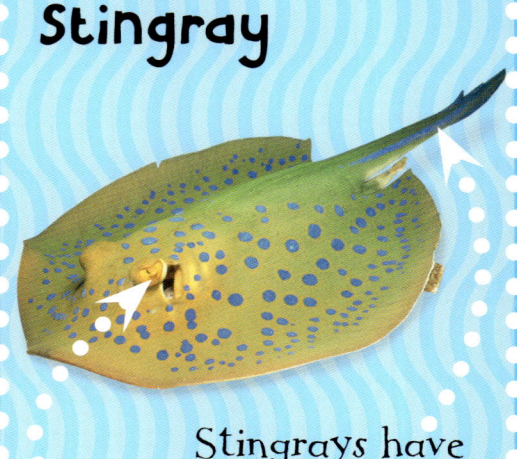

eye

Stingrays have poisonous spines in their tail.

Jellyfish

Jellyfish have no heart, no blood, and no brain!

tentacles

Tropical fish

percula clown fish

butterfly fish

regal fish

coral

Sea turtle

flipper

shell

head

Sea turtles can live for up to 80 years.

Shark

Sharks have several rows of teeth. New teeth are growing all the time.

snout

eye

Squid

Squid have eight **arms**.

Lobster

Lobsters have strong claws, which they use to break open shellfish.

hard shell

Starfish

Starfish live on the sea floor.

leg

claw

antenna

fin

tail fin

dorsal (back) fin

Animals in danger

Many animals are in danger of becoming extinct. This means that there are very few left alive, and they may die out.

Jaguar

Jaguars are in danger because so many people hunt them.

Macaw

Some types of parrot are in danger because people catch them to sell as pets.

curved beak

long tail feathers

Nature reserves

Some animals, like this elephant, live in special places called nature reserves, where they are protected from hunters and other damage caused by humans.

thick, tough skin

strong leg

Whale

For many years there have been laws limiting the hunting of whales. Several types of whale are still in danger. Some, like the humpback whale, are beginning to recover.

Giant panda

There are only about 1,000 wild pandas left alive. They all live in the mountains in China.

dark eye patches

thick coat

Polar bear

Because of climate change, warm air is damaging the icy places where polar bears and seals live.

A **thick coat** keeps the polar bear warm in the cold.

Gorilla

Farmers and loggers are taking the land on which the gorillas live. People also hunt gorillas.

Rhinoceros

Rhinoceroses are in danger because too many people hunt them for their horns.

thick skin

horn

Tiger

Tigers are in danger because loggers and road-builders are damaging the places in which the tigers live.

long whiskers

Every tiger has a different pattern of **stripes**.

In space

The Earth is one of eight planets that travel through space around the Sun. The Sun and the eight planets make up the solar system.

Day and night

The Sun shines on half the Earth at any one time. When it shines on the part where you are, it is day. When it is day on your half of the Earth, it is night on the other half.

day   night

Earth and its moon

The Earth spins as it goes around the Sun. It takes 24 hours (one day and one night) to spin around once.

moon

Sun

Earth

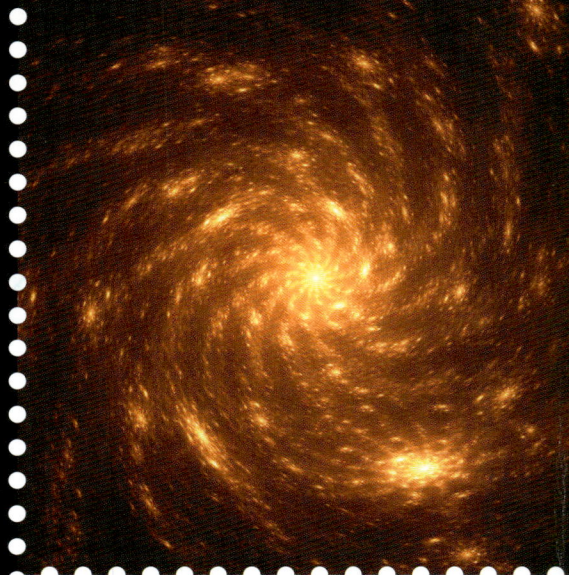

The moon travels around the Earth. It reflects the Sun's light. The moon takes more than 27 days to travel round the Earth.

Earth's moon

When sunlight hits the whole of the face of the moon that we see from Earth, we call it a **full moon**.

The solar system

Jupiter

Uranus

Earth

Mercury

Neptune

Saturn

Mars

Venus

Sun

Galaxies

Our Sun is just one of thousands of stars. Groups of stars are called galaxies. The galaxy we live in is called the **Milky Way**. Galaxies come in different shapes. Spiral galaxies have curving arms.

Stars in the night sky

If you live in the southern half of the Earth, you can see the **southern cross**.

If you live in the northern half of the Earth, you can see the **plough**.

Sometimes we see a **half moon**, when the Sun lights up only half of the surface that is facing Earth.

When the part of the moon lit by sunlight faces mainly away from Earth, we see a **crescent moon**.

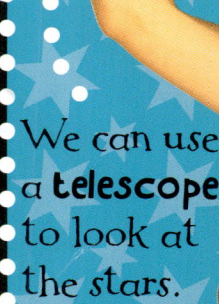

We can use a **telescope** to look at the stars.

35

Continents and oceans

The world contains seven continents or large blocks of land. The seven continents cover only one third of the world's surface. The rest is ocean.

Europe

Europe contains the beautiful city of Paris, in France.

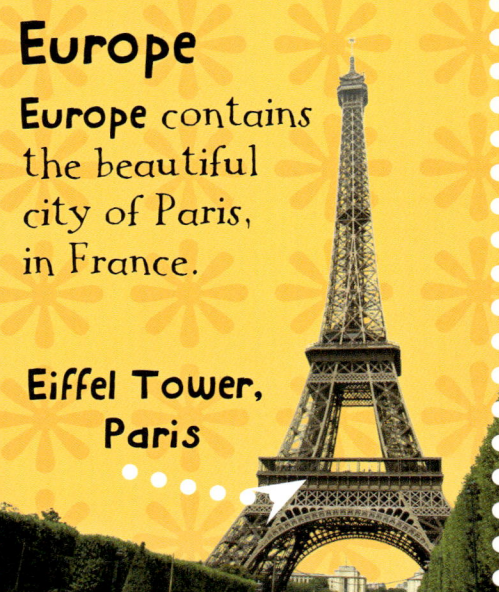

Eiffel Tower, Paris

Africa

Africa contains the world's biggest desert – the Sahara.

sand dunes in the Sahara Desert

North America

Canada, Mexico and the United States are all part of **North America.**

skyscrapers in New York City

South America

South America contains the vast Amazonian rainforest.

tree frog

North America

Europe

Pacific Ocean

Atlantic Ocean

South America

Africa

Antarctica

Asia

China is in Asia. More people live in China than in any other country in the world.

The Great Wall of China

Oceans

There are five main oceans – the Pacific, the Atlantic, the Indian, the Arctic and the Southern Oceans. The Pacific is the largest of these.

dolphins playing in the Pacific Ocean

Australia and Oceania

Australia, New Zealand and many Pacific islands are part of this continent.

Uluru, Australia

Antarctica

Almost the whole continent of **Antarctica** is covered with thick ice.

seal in Antarctica

Arctic Ocean

Asia

Pacific Ocean

Indian Ocean

Southern Ocean

Australia and Oceania

Volcanoes

A volcano is a hole in the Earth's surface. When hot liquid rock spills out through the hole, we say the volcano is erupting. The liquid rock is called lava.

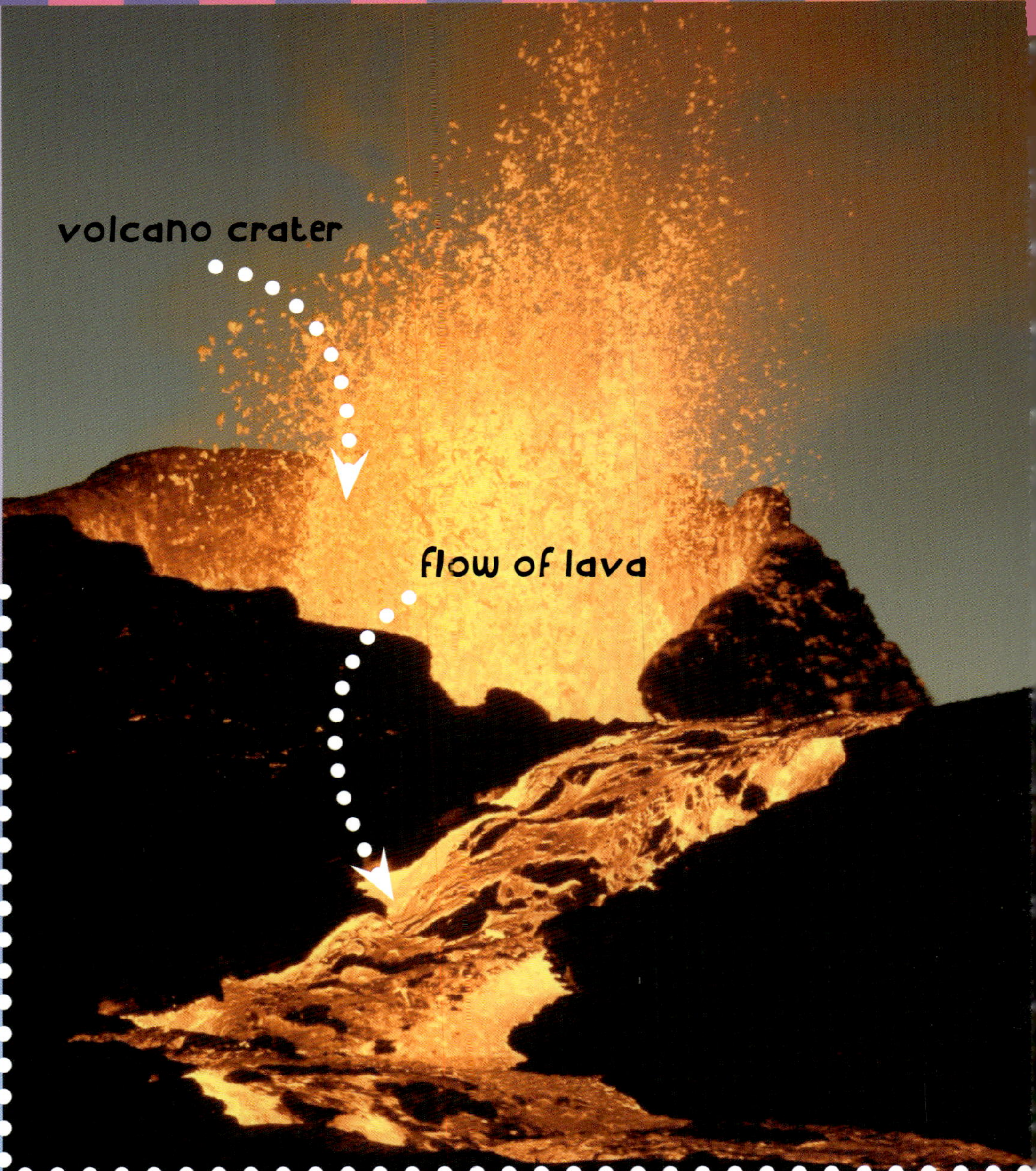

Fertile land

The land near volcanoes is usually very good for growing food.

volcano crater

flow of lava

flames

smoke

What's inside

The top layer of the Earth's surface is the **crust**. Beneath the hard crust is liquid **molten rock**. In the centre is the **solid core**.

solid core

crust

molten rock

Earthquakes

The Earth's crust has split into large pieces called plates. When they move, they cause an earthquake. In a large earthquake, roads crumble and buildings fall down.

Tsunamis

An earthquake under the sea can create a giant wave called a tsunami. When it hits land, a tsunami can cause terrible damage.

Landslides

In a landslide, rock and earth come loose and fall down the side of a mountain or hill. Landslides are caused by earthquakes, and sometimes also by floods from overflowing rivers or heavy rainfall.

crack in road

The Earth's landscapes

Some parts of the Earth are hot and dry, others are cold and icy. Some areas are rocky and sandy, while in other places many plants grow.

Rivers and lakes

dragonfly

Green plants grow beside rivers and lakes. Many insects and birds find their food there or in the water.

mallard ducks

Seashore

Waves shape the land along the seashore. They make softer rocks crumble and move sand up and down the beach.

cliffs

waves

You find trees, grasses and other plants on tops of cliffs and in fields behind the beach.

Snow and ice

It is so cold in the Arctic and the Antarctic that the sea sometimes freezes! The Arctic is in the far north of the Earth and the Antarctic is in the far south.

ice

seals

Mountains

High in the mountains, it is often cold and icy. It can be hard for animals to find grass on the rocky slopes.

Meadowland

On a sunny day, you'll see butterflies fluttering above the meadow flowers. Rabbits, voles and other animals are busy in the grasses round about.

spotted hyena

Rainforest

In the rainforest, snakes hide in the thick green grass. It is a noisy place – you can hear the roar of a waterfall as well as the chatter of monkeys and birds high in the trees.

Deserts and grasslands

Few plants can grow in deserts and dusty grasslands, but animals like the leopard can survive on dry plains.

Seasons

In many parts of the world, there are four seasons in every year. They are spring, summer, autumn and winter. They bring different types of weather.

palm tree

coral

Spring

In spring, the days grow longer and the weather becomes warmer. There are often showers of rain. The trees blossom and produce new leaves. Birds and animals often have babies.

pink blossom

duckling

birds' nest

Polar climate

Near the North and South Poles, there are only two seasons – a long, cold winter and a short, cool summer.

king penguin

Tropical climate

Near the equator – in the parts of the earth farthest away from the poles – it is hot all year round. Some countries here are nearly always dry. In others there are two seasons, one hot and wet and one hot and dry.

Summer

In summer, the days are long and the weather is hotter than at other times of year. The leaves are green, and many plants flower and produce delicious fruits.

Autumn

The days become shorter in autumn. Leaves turn orange and brown and fall off the trees. There are often storms and windy weather. In some countries, people harvest foods.

Winter

In winter, the weather is colder than at other times of year, and the days are short. Many trees have bare branches. When the air is very cold, the water in rainclouds freezes. It falls as snow.

raspberry

strawberry

sunflower

green leaves

orange-brown leaves

pumpkin

squirrel

acorns

snowman

snow and frost on the branches

Weather

Different kinds of weather change how we feel and how the world around us looks. Extreme types of weather like hurricanes or floods can be dangerous.

Very heavy rain can cause a **flood**.

Blizzards are storms of cold winds, snow and ice.

Rainy

When it rains, drops of water fall from clouds in the sky. Getting wet is uncomfortable, but we need rain to make plants grow. Dark clouds are heavy with water – you know it's going to pour. Remember your raincoat and your umbrella!

raincoat

umbrella

Snowy

When the air is very cold, raindrops fall as icy snowflakes. If it is snowy, you need to wear a thick coat, gloves and a hat.

A **drought** is when there is no rain. Trees and plants can die.

Sunny

On a sunny day in summer, we wear light clothes. Too much sunlight is not good for you – wear a hat and have sunscreen on your face and body.

44

Lightning bolts are flashes of electricity in storm clouds.

Stormy

Storms usually bring winds and heavy rain, and sometimes loud thunder and flashes of lightning. You need to wear boots and a waterproof coat.

Foggy

When it is foggy, the air is full of tiny drops of water. You may feel cold, and your clothes will get damp if you don't wear a coat.

Windy

The wind is air moving about. Winds can be strong enough to blow down trees. A light wind is called a breeze.

Hurricanes are storms of whirling wind. They can rip buildings apart.

Religions

Many people have a religion. They worship a god or gods, and follow teachings on how to live. Each religion has its own holy books.

Christianity

Christians worship one God. At Christmas they celebrate the birth of God's son, Jesus Christ, who lived on Earth 2,000 years ago. They worship in a church.

Buddhism

Buddhists follow the teachings of an Indian prince, the Buddha, who lived on Earth 2,500 years ago. They worship in a temple. Some Buddhists like to hang prayer flags outside their homes.

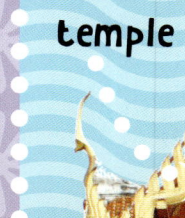

prayer flag

temple

The Christians' holy book is the **Bible.**

Buddhist monks live peacefully together in monasteries.

Judaism

Jews worship God in a synagogue. Their religion is Judaism. In many of their festivals – like Pesach (Passover) each spring – they remember important events in their long history.

The Jewish holy book is the **Torah**. Jews read from it in the synagogue.

Buddhists try to train their minds by sitting quietly in meditation. Statues of the **Buddha** often show him sitting in meditation.

At **Hannukah** (the Festival of Lights), Jews light candles in a special candlestick, the **Menorah**.

Islam

Muslims worship one God, Allah. They follow the teachings of the Prophet Mohammed, who lived on Earth 1,400 years ago. Their religion is called Islam. They are taught to pray five times every day.

Muslims worship in a **mosque**. From the towers (or minarets) criers call people to prayer.

Hinduism

Hindus worship many gods and goddesses. They usually see them as different forms of one God. Their holy books are called the Vedas. Some Hindus believe that God is in everything that exists.

Muslims bow to the ground when they **pray**.

The Muslims' holy book is the **Koran**.

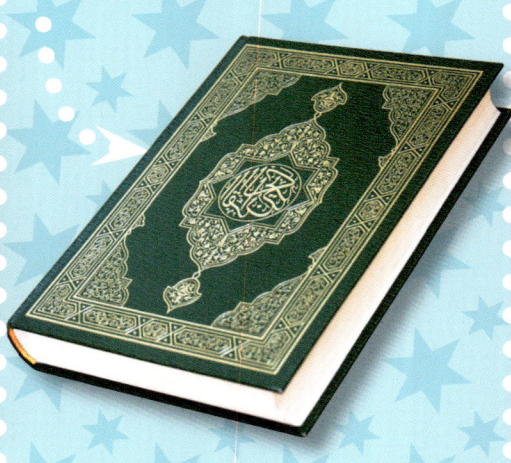

Hindus worship at home or in a temple called a **mandir**.

Some Muslims have strict rules and say that girls and women should cover themselves up. Some Muslim women wear long clothes and a **veil** across their face.

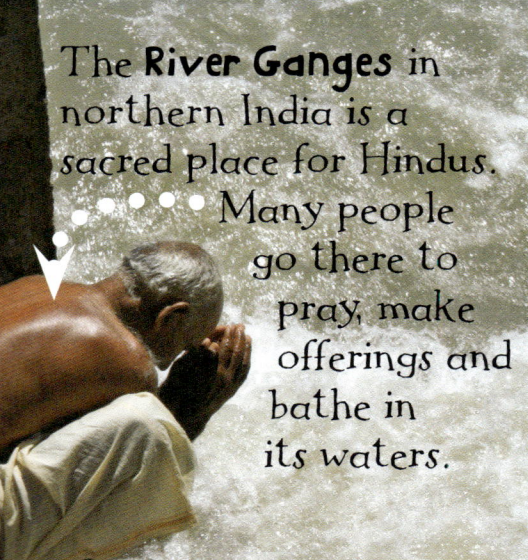

The **River Ganges** in northern India is a sacred place for Hindus. Many people go there to pray, make offerings and bathe in its waters.

Sikhism

Sikhs worship one God. They follow the teachings of ten gurus or teachers. The first was Guru Nanak, who lived in India about 500 years ago. Sikhs worship God by meditating on His name, Waheguru.

At temple, Sikhs share food in a kitchen called a langar.

statues of gods and godesses

Sikh men and boys wear a **turban**, a kind of headscarf. This is because they don't have haircuts. They wear their hair long, wound up beneath the turban. Sikh girls and women also have long hair. They often wear it loose or gathered in a bun.

The holiest place for Sikhs is the **Golden Temple** in Amritsar, India. Sikhs travel there on a religious journey called a pilgrimage.

Festivals

At festivals, people often have parties with music. Some festivals mark a religious day. Others celebrate the season or a major event in a country's history.

Ramadan and Eid ul-Fitr

In the holy month of Ramadan, Muslims give up eating and drinking during the day. At the end they celebrate in **Eid ul-Fitr**. They share special meals and sweets and give children gifts.

4 July

On 4 July people in the United States have parades, barbecues, picnics and firework displays. They celebrate the day in 1776 when their country declared itself independent of – or free from – Great Britain.

Easter

At Easter, Christians celebrate that Jesus Christ came back to life after he was put to death on a cross. They make gifts of Easter eggs as signs of new life.

hand-painted Easter egg

United States flag

picnic basket

Mardi Gras

Mardi Gras is a big party to mark the last days before Lent. During Lent, Christians prepare for Easter with a quiet life and prayers. At Mardi Gras, or Carnival, there are famous parties in New Orleans in the United States and Rio de Janeiro in Brazil. People often wear masks.

feather mask

fancy dress for a Mardi Gras parade

New Year

Chinese people have a great time at New Year. They put up displays of lanterns, hold colourful parades and watch dancers in dragon costumes.

dragon headdress

Diwali

Hindus light clay lamps to celebrate Diwali (the Festival of Lights). People make curved rangoli patterns with coloured sand. They paint red and white footprints in their homes and let off fireworks.

Music

It feels good to sing or play music in a group. It's also fun to listen while other people play or sing. But be prepared – the music may make you want to dance!

Strings

You play a violin or cello by moving a bow across the strings.

cello

bridge

violin

bow

chin rest

tuning peg

All together

People often play the guitar while singing songs with their friends.

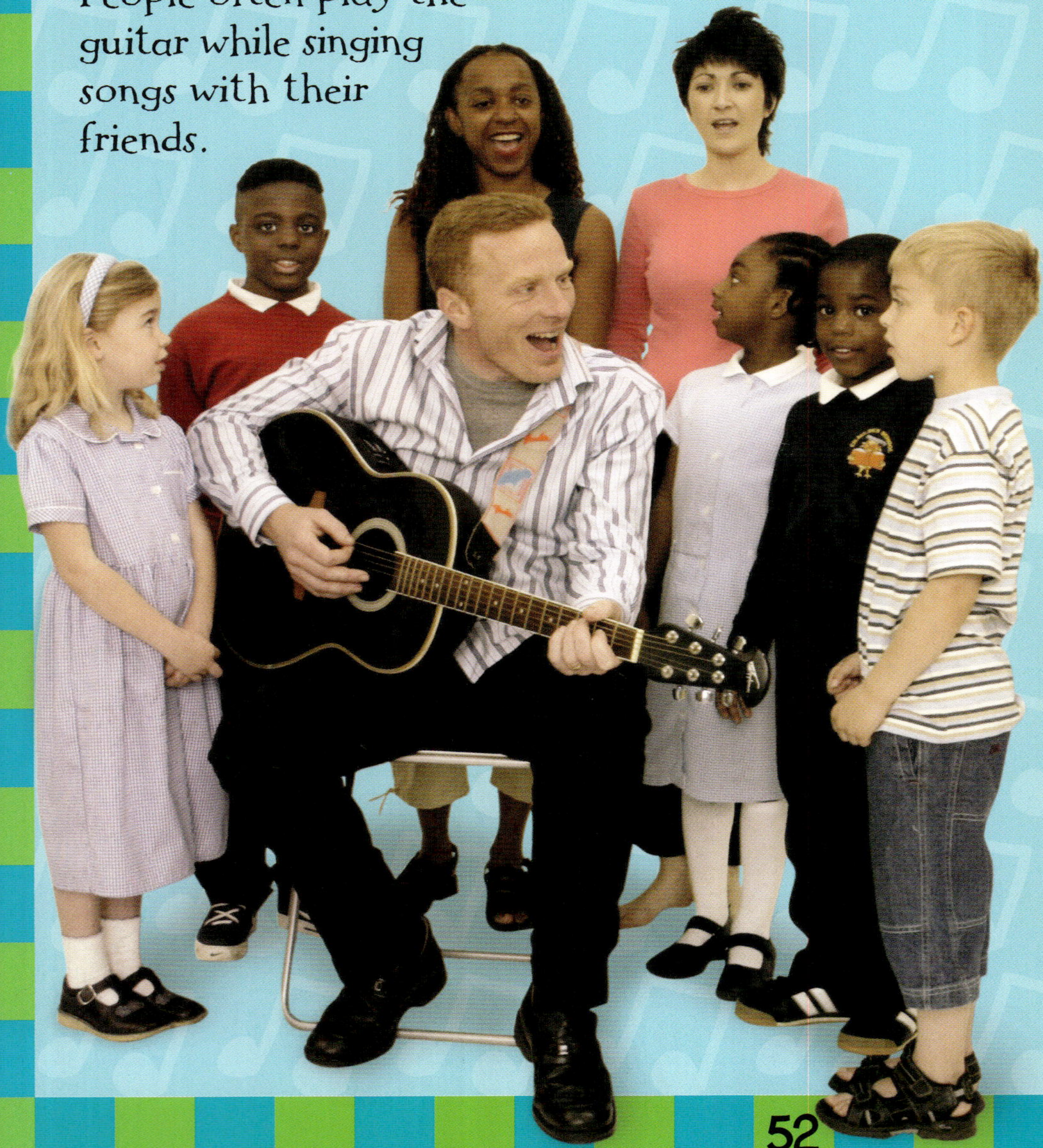

Guitar

You pluck or strum the strings to play music on the guitar.

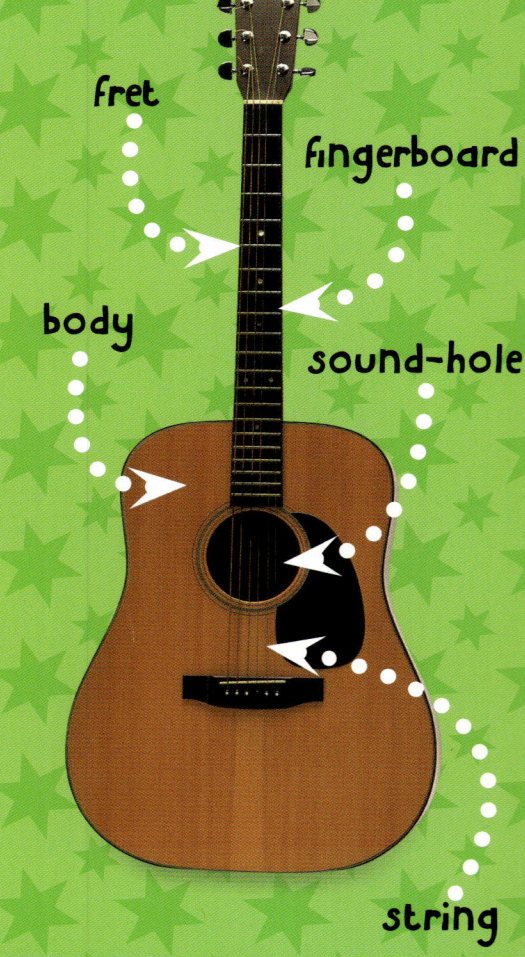

fret

fingerboard

body

sound-hole

string

Singing

You can make lovely music with your voice.

microphone

Keyboard

On a piano or organ you press keys to make the instrument play.

Wind

You have to blow into some instruments to make them play.

reed

saxophone

valve

trumpet

recorder

Percussion

If you have a percussion instrument, you make music by shaking or banging.

drum

triangle

tambourine

xylophone

Entertainment

When it's time to relax, people enjoy reading, listening to music and watching films. It's also fun to entertain yourself by dancing or putting on theatre shows.

Indoor games

There are several games that are good to play at home. How many do you know?

Dance

Ballet is a beautiful form of dance. Dancing makes your muscles strong.

Writing

In English we use the 26 letters of the alphabet, a z. Other languages have different letters.

Hebrew letters

a b c d e f g h i
j k l m n o p q r
s t u v w x y z

Books and stories

In comics and illustrated books, writers use pictures and words to tell stories. Older children and grown-ups often like to read books that only have words.

You make shapes with your body

Ballet dancers wear tights

Theatre

Get out some old clothes and put on a theatre show. When you're acting, you can be anyone you want to be!

Television and computers

Many people relax by watching cartoons, films and dramas on television. On a computer you can play games and talk to your friends by email or instant messaging.

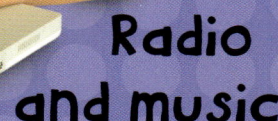

Film

You can watch films on TV or a computer, but it's really exciting to see them on a big screen in a cinema. It's great fun to go there with your friends. Maybe your mum or dad will buy you some popcorn!

cinema tickets

Radio and music

People love to listen to music on the go. They use small radios or music players. The music plays in their ears through earphones. On the radio there are talkshows as well as music.

earphones

Puppet theatre

Puppet shows are a fun kind of theatre. The controller puts her hand inside the glove puppets to make them move.

Jobs

When you grow up, you choose a job. In some jobs, you look after people. In others, you grow or make food, build things or entertain people.

Baker

Do you like an iced bun as a treat? As well as cakes, bakers make the bread loaves you eat every day.

Nurse

Nurses work with doctors in hospitals. They look after people who are sick or injured.

first-aid case

patrol car

radio

Doctor

You visit the doctor when you don't feel well. The doctor finds out what is wrong.

Police officer

Police officers patrol the streets, either on foot or in cars. Their job is to keep people safe. They use a radio to stay in touch with the police station.

Brightly coloured waterproof trousers

Teacher

At school, your teacher helps you learn to write, read, add up – and many other fun things.

pupil

Firefighter

Firefighters come very quickly in their fire truck when there is a fire. They put out the flames with streams of water.

helmet

face mask

fire truck

Musician

Musicians practise every day so they can play or sing well in concerts.

recorder

Construction worker

Construction workers build roads and buildings. They wear bright jackets so they can be seen.

hard hat

tools

Ballet dancer

Ballet dancers wear special shoes so they can dance on their toes. They have a stiff dress called a tutu that looks pretty when they are dancing.

ballet shoes

tutu

Travellers and explorers

In the past many explorers went on great journeys to find new lands. Today travellers set out on difficult trips because they want adventure.

Poles

American explorer Robert Peary led the first trip to reach the North Pole, in 1909. Roald Amundsen of Norway was the first man to reach the South Pole, in 1911.

Skis make it easier to travel over snow.

Moon landing

On 21 July 1969, American astronaut Neil Armstrong became the first man to walk on our moon. He flew there on the Apollo 11 spacecraft.

The United States flag.

Armstrong left footprints on the moon's surface.

Australia

Aborigines have lived in Australia for 30,000 years. The first Europeans found it in the 1700s.

Vikings

About 1,000 years ago Vikings from Norway, Sweden and Denmark seized land all over northern Europe. They were fierce fighters, who sailed in longships.

The highest mountain

In 1953 Edmund Hillary and Tenzing Norgay were the first people to climb Mount Everest. Everest is 29,035 feet (8,850 metres) tall – the world's highest mountain. It is right on the border between Nepal and Tibet.

Pacific Islanders

About 30,000 years ago, people from Asia began to explore the islands in the Pacific Ocean. They sailed a very long way in light canoes. Today their descendants – the Pacific Islanders – live on thousands of islands in the Pacific Ocean.

Camels can carry people or bags of goods.

From Italy to China by camel

Italian merchant Marco Polo travelled across land, mainly by camel, from Italy to China in 1271–75. He wrote a book, **The Travels of Marco Polo**, to tell Europeans about life in Asia.

Discovering America

In 1492, Italian sailor Christopher Colombus tried to sail to Asia from Europe by going west instead of east. He discovered America!

Getting around

You can get around using your own energy – on a bicycle or in a canoe. To go longer distances, people use machines like cars and trains.

Aircraft

You can often travel a long way very cheaply in an airliner.

light aircraft

airliner

Motorboat

Large motorboats like this one have comfortable cabins.

Helicopter

blade

Helicopters can take off from or land on the flat top of a building.

Hot-air balloon

basket

Large cruise liners have lots of **decks**.

Cruise liner

Yacht

A yacht will speed across the sea if you catch the wind in its sails.

sail

Canoe

You need to wear a **life jacket** when you go out in a canoe.

Bicycle

Make sure you wear a helmet when you go out on your bike.

Car

Most cars need petrol, but some new ones run partly on electricity.

windscreen

headlamp

Bus

It's good fun to travel by bus with all your friends!

mirror

flashing lights

bumper

Tractor

Farmers need tractors to get across muddy fields.

thick tyre

Train

Going by train is quick and easy.

Delivering and rescuing

Police, fire and ambulance crews arrive very quickly in their special vehicles. Big trucks and freight trains carry things a long way.

Freight train

Some of the world's biggest trains carry goods across country.

diesel engine

freight car

Police launch

The police use boats like this launch on rivers and at sea.

Delivery van

There's plenty of room in the back of this delivery van for carrying parcels and large pieces of equipment about.

lights

Police car

Police drivers are good at driving safely while going very fast.

131

9747

WE SERVE AND PROTECT

CHICAGO POLICE

Fire truck

The fire truck carries the firefighters and the equipment they need to put out fires.

The **firefighters** travel in the cab.

Equipment is stored in the back part of the truck.

Truck

radiator grill

exhaust pipe

Police motorcycle

On his motorcycle, the policeman can zoom along roads crowded with cars.

helicopter ambulance

Medicines and **equipment** are stored in the back part of the ambulance.

Ambulance

Ambulances have to get to an accident as quickly as possible to help injured people.

INDEX

animals 24-25, 26-27, 28-29, 30-31, 32-33, 40-41, 42-43
animals in danger 32-33
arteries 6

balanced diet 14-15, 16-17
birds 21, 25, 40-41
blood 6-7, 8
body 4-5, 6-7, 8-9, 10-11, 12-13, 14-15, 16-17
bones 4-5, 14, 17
books 54
brain 4-5, 10, 11
breathing 6, 13, 20

cleanliness 14-15
climates 42-43
computers 55
continents 36-37
creepy-crawlies 24

dancing 52, 54, 57
deserts 41
digestion 7, 17
dizzyness 11
drinking 15, 17

ears 11
Earth 34-35, 38-39, 40-41
earthquakes 39
eating see food
entertainment 54-55, 56
exercise 14, 17
exploration 58-59
eyes 10

families 18-19
farm animals 27
festivals 50-51
films 55
fingerprints 8
fingers 8
fish 30-31
flowers 20-21, 22
food 12-13, 14-15, 16-17, 20-21, 56
fruit 23

galaxy 35
games 54-55
germs 8, 15
glasses 10
God, gods 46-47, 48-49, 50-51
grasslands 41

hair 9, 13
health 14-15, 16-17
hearing see ears
heart 6, 14

insects 21, 24, 40-41
intestines 7

jobs 56-57
joints 4

kidneys 7
lakes 40

landscapes 40-41
landslides 39
liver 7
lungs 6

martial arts 14
meadowlands 41
melanin 8
Milky Way 35
mind 5, 14
moon 34-35
mountains 41
muscles 4-5, 6, 14
music 52-53, 54-55, 57

nerves 4-5, 10, 11, 13
nose 13
nostrils 13
nuts 21, 22

oceans 36-37
organs 4
oxygen 6

pets 26
planets 34-35
plants 20-21, 22-23, 40-41, 42-43, 44
problems 15

radio 55
rainforest 41
reflex action 5
religions 46-47, 48-49, 50-51
rest 14-15
ribcage 4
rivers 40

sea animals 30-31
seashore 40-41
seasons 42-43
seeds 20-21, 22
seeing see eyes

senses 10-11, 12-13
skin 8, 13, 15, 44
skull 4
sleep 14-15
smelling see nose
snow and ice 40
solar system 34-35
space 34-35
spiders 24
spinal cord 5
stars 35
stomach 7
stories 54
Sun 34-35
sweating 8

taste buds 12
tasting see tongue, nose
teeth 7, 15
television 55
tendons 5
theatre 55
thinking 5
tongue 12
transport 60-61, 62-63
travel 58-59, 60-61, 62-63
trees 22-23
tsunamis 39

volcanoes 38

weather 42-43, 44-45
wild animals 28-29
worship 46-47, 48-49, 50-51
writing 54

X-rays 4